Anastasia

Anastasia
The Movie Novel

Adapted by Cathy East Dubowski

A Don Bluth / Gary Goldman Film

HarperActive™

A Division of HarperCollinsPublishers

To my parents,
Bill and Bobbie East,
who gave me the gifts
of love, language, and laughter

Prologue

Marie's Tale
St. Petersburg, Russia, 1916

A night to remember . . .

We all said it would be a night to remember.

And it was.

But not as we had dreamed. No one could have imagined the events that would befall us.

I am the Dowager Empress Marie of Russia. And it was the worst night of my long life.

But let me start at the beginning. . . .

There was a time, not very long ago, when we lived in an enchanted world. A world of elegant palaces and grand parties.

The year was 1916. My son Nicholas was the Czar of Imperial Russia. He and his wife had four beautiful daughters and a handsome young son.

Nicholas was a good man. But some have said he did not rule wisely. Some have said he was blind to the poverty and hunger that tore at his people.

I do not know. I only know that he was a good son and a loving father.

The stars shone brightly that night as my carriage raced through the darkness. The horses' hooves clattered on the cobblestone streets. The light from the palace lit up the night as the gates swung open for my carriage. I joined the guests, who were dressed in their finest suits and gowns.

We were celebrating a special anniversary. Three hundred years of Romanov rule. And that night, no star burned brighter than my youngest granddaughter, our sweet Anastasia.

All eyes were on her as she danced with her father, the Czar. Her long red curls shone in the light from the chandelier. She was only eight, but she danced with spirit and grace.

When the dance ended, she curtsied to her father. Then she saw me. Laughing, she ran into my arms.

Why were the two of us so close? I do not know. Perhaps she reminded me of myself at her age. We were the best of friends.

But I was leaving. She had begged me not to return to my home in Paris. So I had a very special gift made for her. I hoped it would make it easier for us to say good-bye.

Smiling, I pulled the gift from my bag.

"For me?" Anastasia said as she reached for the tiny box. "Is it a jewelry box?"

I shook my head. "Look."

I held up a key: a small flower on a gold neck chain. I showed her how to fit it into the tiny hole at the back of the box. Then I wound it.

A haunting melody played.

Anastasia clapped her hands. "It plays our lullaby!"

"You can play it at night before you go to sleep," I told her. "You can pretend I am singing to you."

And then I sang to her the words that would haunt me for years to come:

> *"On the wind, 'cross the sea,*
> *Hear this song and remember,*
> *Soon you'll be home with me*
> *Once upon a December . . ."*

I handed Anastasia the key. "Read what it says."
Anastasia peered at the tiny letters engraved on

the key. "'Together in Paris,'" she read. Then she looked at me with her beautiful blue eyes. "Really?"

I smiled and nodded.

"Oh, Grandmama!" She threw her sweet young arms around my neck. We hugged as if we would never let go.

Suddenly a startled gasp rose from the crowd. The orchestra stopped playing. The laughter died. Anastasia and I spun around.

The crowd parted like dry leaves before a wind.

A man swept toward us—an uninvited guest. He was tall and thin, dressed in long black robes. His gleaming black mustache and beard hung below his waist.

Someone in the crowd stifled a cry as a small white bat swooped above our heads and landed on the man's shoulder.

Slowly the man made his way to the Czar. His hypnotic eyes blazed with anger beneath thick black brows.

Nicholas met his gaze, unafraid.

"You think you can banish the Great Rasputin?" the man cried. His lips curled into a sneer. "By the unholy powers vested in me, I banish you! Mark my words: You and your family will die within the fortnight."

Anastasia clung to me as Rasputin's curse echoed through the great ballroom: "I will not rest until I see the end of the Romanov line . . . forever!"

Then I noticed a strange object hanging from a chain around Rasputin's waist. Looking closer, I saw that it was a reliquary—a fancy glass vial about eight inches tall. Its contents glowed like devil's fire.

Eyes crazed, Rasputin raised the reliquary and muttered a few words. A bolt of lightning shot into the chandelier, and it crashed to the floor. Guests scattered as the ballroom plunged into darkness.

The servants rushed to light candles around the room.

Anastasia and I trembled in each other's arms until the soft glow of candlelight filled the room. I looked around.

Rasputin had vanished.

No one danced another step that night. Rasputin had stolen our joy.

❁

That night as I got ready for bed, I heard an angry crowd of demonstrators outside the palace gates. "Death to the Czar!" they shouted. "Let the people rule!"

A brick shattered an elegant palace window.

Rasputin, I thought. Some said he practiced black

magic. Some said he was the devil himself. Did he have a hand in the terror of those events? I never knew for sure.

I only know that the spark of unhappiness in our country was fanned into flames—flames that would destroy our lives forever.

❀

Later that night I awoke to a loud knocking. I flung back my satin covers and hurried to my bedroom door.

A servant had come to warn me: revolutionaries had broken through the gates. They had toppled a statue of the Czar. Now they were trying to break into the palace. They meant to kill the royal family.

The next thing I knew, we were all running down a darkened hallway. There was no time even to dress.

I clutched the hand of the sleepy Anastasia as we ran. But suddenly she stopped, pulling her hand free. "My music box!" she cried. She turned back to get it.

I tried to stop her. But she was so like her father— as stubborn as a black bear. As I ran after her, I wished to heaven that I had never given her the tiny music box. For now she was risking her life for it.

"Anastasia!" I begged. "Anastasia, come back!"

But she would not listen.

At last I found her in her room, hugging the music box to her chest. Before I could speak, shots rang out—inside the palace!

I whispered a prayer as I reached for my granddaughter's hand.

Suddenly a secret panel in the wall slid open. Out stepped a young servant boy.

The castle was full of secret passageways. Nicholas himself had played hide-and-seek in them as a child.

Now my granddaughter and I ran to hide in them, but this time it was not a game. We were running for our lives.

"This way!" the boy urged us.

My old bones creaked as I ducked through the doorway. "Hurry, Anastasia!" I scolded. Fear made my voice harsher than I meant it to be.

Then the boy thrust Anastasia in behind me. I forgave his rudeness in shoving the Princess, given the danger we were in. But in his haste he caused her to drop the music box.

Her hand shot out to grab it—just as Bartok, Rasputin's white bat, swooped into the room and saw us.

"Rasputin, they're getting away!" the creature shrieked as it flew off to find its master.

That's when I realized we were being hunted not only by the revolutionaries, but by Rasputin as well!

"Go, go!" the boy shouted. He slammed the secret panel shut behind us.

Frozen in fear, we paused in the darkness and listened.

Heavy footsteps rang out as angry revolutionaries stormed into the room.

We heard a loud slap. "Where are they, boy?"

"They're not here," he replied.

Such bravery, I thought, *in a boy so young*.

Then we heard a thumping noise and a sharp cry. It sounded as if the man had struck the poor boy with his rifle.

I covered Anastasia's mouth with my hand to stifle her gasp. There was no way to help the boy, no time to thank him. I dragged the Princess away down the dark passage.

❂

We escaped from the palace through the servants' entrance and fled into the frosty darkness. We had not run far when a dazzling light lit up the night. I glanced over my shoulder.

The palace was in flames!

I had no idea where my son and the rest of his family had gone. I only knew I must save Anastasia.

We dashed toward the river, shivering in our thin nightgowns. The water had frozen over, and we slipped on the ice as we raced beneath the bridge. My old heart beat out the precious seconds as we ran.

Suddenly I heard Anastasia scream. I whirled around.

Rasputin had found us! He jumped from the bridge and landed hard on the ice. Cracks spread out like spiderwebs around his dark body as he grabbed Anastasia by the ankle.

She screamed again. "Let me go!"

Rasputin's laughter rumbled like midnight thunder. "You'll never escape me, child. NEVER!"

Then the ice beneath him broke with a terrifying *CRACK!*

I gasped in horror. Surely they would both drown!

But just as the river nearly swallowed them, Anastasia wrenched herself free with a shout. She scrambled across the ice and fell gasping upon the bank.

The child glanced back. Rasputin's furious red gaze seemed to hypnotize her. I feared she would rise and go to him. Then she pulled her eyes free, lurched to her feet, and ran.

"Bartok!" Rasputin screamed as he dug his fingernails into the ice. Then the river's swift current sucked him down into the freezing waters.

The glowing reliquary skittered across the ice. Bartok, the white bat, swooped down and scooped it up, then disappeared into the dark night.

❁

At last we made our way to the train station. We were freezing, frightened, and cared nothing for how foolish we must have looked running through the streets in our nightgowns and coats.

All around us hundreds of other terrified people shoved to get on the train. I gripped Anastasia's hand with all my strength as I forced our way through the crowd. "Hurry, Anastasia," I panted.

The whistle blew. The train jerked and slowly began to chug down the track. It couldn't leave without us!

I reached up, begging for help. Passengers on the packed train grabbed my hands. My arms ached as they pulled me upward. I nearly wept with relief.

"Grandmama!"

I looked around. Anastasia! Where was she?

And then I saw her. She was still running alongside the train! Desperately I reached for her. "Hold on to my hand!"

Our fingertips touched. Then I felt her hand grip mine.

"Don't let go!" she cried.

I held on tightly as I gazed down into her fright-ened young face. But an old woman's arms are not very strong. The train began to chug faster and faster out of the station. "Help me!" I begged the others around me.

But then I felt her small hand slip from my grasp.

"Anastasia!" I screamed.

Horrified, I watched her stumble and fall. Her head struck the platform. And then she lay still.

"Anastasia!"

I tried to jump from the fast-moving train, but strong hands held me back. I suppose they feared I would be killed if I jumped. Perhaps I might have, but all I wanted to do was help my granddaughter. I fought, but they would not let me go.

They did not know who I was, or who I had left behind.

I stared at my dear granddaughter, Russia's youngest princess, lying helpless on the dirty ground.

And then a sea of people swirled around her, and I could see her no more.

❀

So many lives were destroyed that night. What had always been was now gone forever. And my Anastasia, my beloved granddaughter . . . would I ever see her again?

Chapter One

Ten years later

It was a gray winter day. Deep snow froze the toes of the people who stood in long lines, hoping to buy bread.

It had been ten long years since the Revolution swept through their homeland. The Czar and his family had been murdered. The new government promised food and wealth and a new way of life.

Still, the people starved. Still, they lived in poverty. Freedom was a fading dream.

"Thank goodness for gossip!" one woman said to another in line. "It's what gets me through the day."

A man in front of her turned around. "Have you heard? There's a rumor going around St. Petersburg. They say that maybe not all of the Czar's family died."

"They say one daughter may still be alive!" a woman behind her butted in. "The Princess Anastasia!"

"But please do not repeat it!" the man whispered, a look of fear crossing his face.

An old woman drew her tattered coat closer around her neck. "They say her royal grandmama is offering to pay a royal fortune—"

"What for?" a young girl cried.

The old woman's eyes sparkled. "To anyone who can find the Princess and bring her to Paris!"

❂

In another part of the city a young con man named Dimitri carried out his latest scam. He'd rented a small backstreet theater to audition young Russian girls for a very special part.

The role of Anastasia.

Dimitri laid an arm around his stout comrade, his old friend Vladimir. Once Vladimir had been a rich aristocrat. Now he scrounged for a living like everyone else.

But not for much longer, if Dimitri had his way. No more forging papers. No more dealing in stolen goods.

"Everything's going according to plan. All we need is the girl," Dimitri told his friend. "We'll teach her what to say. Then we'll dress her up and take her to Paris. Imagine how much her old grandmama will pay us!" He winked. "Who else could pull it off but you and me?"

"We'll be rich!" Vladimir crowed.

"We'll be out of here!" the young man added.

The auditions went on for hours. But no one was right. At last Dimitri paced the worn wooden floorboards of the stage, studying the last ragtag line of candidates. Each hoped to win the role of Anastasia. Each hoped to share in the reward.

Dimitri shook his head. Not one Anastasia in the whole bunch. Not even close! Even the finest gowns and jewels wouldn't make a difference.

"That's it, Dimitri," Vladimir said, shaking his head. "Our last kopeck gone for this flea-infested theater. And still no girl to play Anastasia."

Dimitri shoved a hand through his thick brown hair. "We'll find her," he said with determination. "She's here somewhere. Maybe right under our noses."

Then Dimitri pulled something from his vest pocket. "Don't forget. One look at this and the Empress will think we've brought the *real* Anastasia."

He gazed at the tiny jeweled box in his hand. For a moment his mind filled with images of the night he'd found it. The night the Revolution began.

He'd been a young servant boy then, working in the palace of the Czar. When the revolutionaries burst through the gates with murder in their eyes, he'd helped two members of the royal family get away.

He remembered a young princess with startling blue eyes and long red curls ducking into the secret passageway. The Empress Marie had escaped to Paris. But what had happened to the girl?

Dimitri shrugged. Who knew? And who cared? No use wondering about her. The days of palaces and princesses were dead. In the past ten years Dimitri had learned the cold, hard facts of life.

There was only one way to survive in this new Russia: by looking out for number one. And Dimitri had had enough.

This new scam—and the tiny jeweled box—were his ticket out.

❁

Off in the countryside, an eighteen-year-old girl named Anya stood by a crooked iron gate and hunched her shoulders against the cold. She made a face at the dreary orphanage that had been her home for the past ten years.

Home. Hardly the word for that place, she

thought.

Oh, the roof had kept out the rain and snow—most of the time. She'd had a place to sleep. The scraps of stale food at least had kept her alive.

But a home meant love and family—things the orphanage didn't give. Anya couldn't remember a time when she'd had either one.

"I got you a job in the fish factory," said the orphanage's fat, balding headmistress. She pointed down the road. "You go straight down this path till you get to the fork in the road. Then go left . . . are you listening?" she snapped.

"I'm listening, Comrade," Anya muttered.

The headmistress scowled. "You've been a thorn in my side ever since you were brought here. Acting like the Queen of Sheba instead of the nameless no-account you are. And for the last ten years I've fed you. I've clothed you. I've—"

"Kept a roof over my head," Anya recited along with her.

The headmistress jammed her fists on her ample hips and glared. "How is it you don't have a clue as to who you were before you came here, but you can remember all that?"

Anya's fingers curled around the gold necklace she always wore. "I *do* have a clue to—"

"Ugh! I know!" The headmistress snatched at the flower-shaped key that hung from Anya's neck. "'Together in Paris.' So you want to go to France to find your family, huh?" The headmistress snickered. "Little Miss Anya, it's time to take your place in life. In life and in line! And be grateful, too!" She slammed the iron gate and waddled back inside.

"'Be grateful,'" Anya muttered as she started off down the snowy road. "Hmph! I *am* grateful. Grateful to get away!"

Soon she came to a fork in the road. Shivering, she stared at the signs. One said FISHERMAN'S VILLAGE and pointed to the left. The other said ST. PETERSBURG and pointed to the right.

Go left, the headmistress had told her. Well, she knew what awaited her to the left. A lifetime spent up to her elbows in stinking fish! There she'd be Anya, the orphan, forever.

But if she chose the path to the right, who knew what could happen?

She touched her necklace. Maybe in St. Petersburg she could find a way to get to Paris. Maybe in Paris she would find out who she was. Who her family had been.

Maybe at last she'd have a home. A *real* home.

Anya closed her eyes and tilted her head toward

the heavens. "Send me a sign," she murmured. "A hint. Anything."

She waited, the cold wind rustling her hair.

All of a sudden she felt a strong tug on her scarf. Her eyes flew open. "Hey!"

A small frisky puppy pranced a few feet away.

"I don't have time to play right now, okay? I'm waiting for a sign." She closed her eyes again.

The puppy ran down the right fork, Anya's scarf flying behind him like a flag. He stopped and barked again.

Anya chased after him and caught the end of her scarf. "Give that back!" She gave the scarf a big yank, and tumbled backward into the snow.

Yap! Yap! The dog sat on his hind legs and waited.

Suddenly it dawned on her. *This* was her sign?

"Oh, great," she muttered. "A *dog* wants me to go to St. Petersburg." She glanced skyward, then shrugged. "Okay. I can take a hint."

With that, Anya flung her scarf around her neck, scooped up the puppy, and took her first uncertain steps toward St. Petersburg—and her future.

Chapter Two

Anya yanked open the heavy door of the Bureau of Bureaucracy. She hurried in from the cold, then stopped dead in her tracks.

The lines of people seemed to stretch on forever.

Anya sighed and took her place in line.

While she waited, she entertained herself by trying to think up a name for her new dog. She'd once found an old book at the orphanage and read about *pookas*—mischievous spirits who could take on many forms.

"You're *my* guiding spirit," Anya said. "So what do you think of the name *Pooka?*"

The puppy barked happily. Anya laughed. "Okay, Pooka it is."

Anya waited and waited. At last it was her turn. "One ticket to Paris, please."

The ticket agent didn't even bother to look up. "Exit visa?"

Anya frowned. "Exit visa?"

"No exit visa, no ticket." Then he hung up a sign—PEOPLE'S LUNCH BREAK—and slammed the shutters in her face.

Now what? Anya thought.

"Pssst!" An old woman shuffled past, bent over her broom. "See Dimitri. He can help."

Anya looked around nervously. "Where can I find him?"

"At the old palace," the woman whispered without looking up. "But you didn't hear it from me."

❁

The once-grand palace rose in the evening sky like a haunted house. Shivering, Anya slipped inside.

"Hello. Anybody home?" When no one answered, she found herself climbing the grand staircase to the second floor.

Anya gazed around her. The place was a wreck! And yet somehow it felt . . . almost friendly.

She smiled as her fingers traced a pattern of dancing bears on a large vase in the corner. She'd always loved this vase—

Wait a minute!

Anya shivered again, but this time it wasn't from the cold. How could she remember a vase she'd never seen? She'd never been inside any palace before, much less the home of the Czar.

"This place . . ." she whispered as she wandered from room to room. "It's like a memory from a dream."

As if her feet knew the way, she soon found herself at the top of a staircase that led down into a huge ballroom.

A life-size painting of the Czar's family covered one wall. Moonlight struck the portrait with a ghostly glow.

The eyes of the Romanovs seemed to speak to her. Anya began to hum a song. A song that often came to her at bedtime, though she could not remember where she'd learned it. *"Once upon a December . . ."*

In her mind's eye, the ballroom appeared as it once had, with gowns and jewels glittering beneath chandeliers. Royal ghosts stepped from the painting and began to waltz.

Anya was safe and warm in someone's arms as

he twirled her around the room. Music, candlelight, smiling faces . . . things her heart used to know and now yearned to remember.

As the music faded, Anya's tall, handsome partner kissed her on the forehead. Her hands held out the skirts of an imaginary gown. She sank into a deep curtsy.

"Once upon a December . . ."

"Hey!" a voice rang out. "What are you doing in here?"

Anya whirled around. Two men—one young, one old—stared at her as if she were a thief. Or crazy. Or both.

Blushing, she ran toward the stairs.

"Hey! Stop!" Dimitri cried. "How did you get in here?"

Anya stopped and turned, caught in a ray of moonlight. The painting of the Romanov family towered behind her.

"Are you Dimitri?" she asked, her blue eyes wide.

Dimitri gasped. The young girl in the painting—Anastasia—stared at him with the same blue eyes.

He shot Vladimir an excited glance.

But he played it cool. "That depends on who wants to know."

"My name is Anya. I need travel papers. I want to go to Paris."

"And who is this here?" Vladimir asked, scooping Pooka into his arms. The puppy licked him. "Oh, look! He likes me."

"Yeah, nice dog," Dimitri said, barely sparing him a glance. "Listen—Anya, was it? Do you have a last name?"

"Well, this is going to sound crazy," Anya mumbled, twisting the end of her scarf. "But I don't know my last name. I was found wandering around when I was eight years old."

Excellent! Dimitri thought. *Anastasia was eight when she disappeared.* "And before that?"

Anya shook her head. "I don't remember. I have very few memories of my past."

"That's perfect," Dimitri whispered to Vladimir. The old aristocrat pulled on his mustache and grinned.

"We're going to Paris ourselves," Dimitri said casually. He patted his vest pocket. "I've got three tickets to Paris right here. But the third one is for her—Anastasia."

Anya frowned. "Anastasia who?"

"Romanov!" Dimitri pointed to the girl in the painting. Was it possible this country bumpkin hadn't heard the rumors?

"We're going to reunite the Grand Duchess Anastasia with her grandmother, the Dowager

Empress Marie," Vladimir explained.

Dimitri rubbed his chin as he strolled around her. "You know, you kind of look like her. The same blue eyes—the Romanov eyes. Nicholas's smile. Alexandra's chin."

Vladimir took her by the hand. "Oh, look! She even has the grandmother's hands."

"She's the same age, too," Dimitri added. "The same physical type."

Anya shook her head, flustered. "Are you trying to tell me you think I am Anastasia?"

Dimitri shrugged. "All I'm trying to tell you is that I've seen thousands of girls all over the country, and not one of them looks as much like the Grand Duchess as you do. I mean, look at the portrait."

Anya began to walk away. "I think you're both mad!"

"Why?" Dimitri asked. "You don't remember what happened to *you*—"

"No one knows what happened to *her*," Vladimir added.

"You're looking for family *in Paris* . . ." Dimitri began.

"And her only family is *in Paris*," Vladimir finished.

"Ever thought about the possibility?" Dimitri asked.

"That I could be royalty?" Anya responded.

They both nodded.

"Well, I don't know," Anya said. "It's kind of hard to think of yourself as a princess when you're sleeping on a cold, hard floor." She gazed at the portrait of the Romanovs. "But yeah, I guess every lonely girl would hope she's a princess."

"And somewhere," Vladimir added, "one girl *is*. After all, the name Anastasia means 'She will rise again.'"

Dimitri had cast his line. The fish—Anya—was about to bite. Now they had to give her some room so they wouldn't scare her off.

"Well, really wish we could help," he said, pulling Vladimir toward the door. "But the third ticket is for the Grand Duchess Anastasia."

"Why didn't you tell her about our brilliant plan?" Vladimir whispered, looking back over his shoulder.

"All she wants to do is go to Paris," Dimitri whispered back. "Why give away a third of the reward money?"

Anya fiddled with the key around her neck as she reached out to touch the portrait. Nicholas, Alexandra, sisters, a brother. Could it be? Dare she hope that this might be her family?

"Dimitri, wait!" Anya cried.

Dimitri jabbed his elbow in Vladimir's round tummy. "Ha! See? Right in the palm of our hand."

Anya ran to catch up with them. "If I don't remember who I am, then who's to say I'm *not* Anastasia. Right?"

"Hmm . . ." Dimitri pretended to ponder the idea. "Go on."

"Yeah, and if I'm not Anastasia," Anya continued, "the Empress will know right away. And it's all just an honest mistake. Right?"

"But if you *are* the Princess," Vladimir said, "then you'll finally know who you are. And you'll have your family back."

Dimitri laughed. "Either way, it gets you to Paris."

"Right!" Anya stuck out her hand. Surprised, Dimitri shook it. "Ow!" For a skinny little orphan, she sure had a mighty strong grip!

Then Dimitri clicked his heels together. "May I present Her Royal Highness, the Grand Duchess Anastasia!"

He and Vladimir bowed. Anya curtsied, then swept Pooka into her arms as she stood up again.

"Pooka!" she told him excitedly. "We're going to Paris!"

"Whoa!" Dimitri said. "Uh . . . the dog stays."

"What are you talking about?" Anya exclaimed. "The dog *goes*."

"No," Dimitri repeated firmly. "The dog does *not* go."

"I say he goes!"

"I'm allergic to dogs!"

Vladimir laughed. Would these two young people bicker all the way to Paris?

Ah, well. It was a small price to pay. For at last they'd found their Anastasia.

❀

Anastasia. The name echoed through the empty ballroom . . .

. . . waking a small white bat.

It was Rasputin's bat, Bartok, who'd lived in the abandoned palace ever since his master had drowned in the river. Next to him Rasputin's reliquary lay wrapped in cobwebs—cold, dark, and lifeless.

"Anastasia?" Bartok shuddered. "Yeah, just one problem there, fella. Anastasia's dead. All the Romanovs are dead, dead, dead."

Anastasia . . . the drafts seemed to swirl the name through the rafters, blowing the dust off the old reliquary.

Anastasia . . .

The reliquary hummed.

Then it shivered to life with an eerie green glow. Smoke began to wisp from the top.

A minion—an evil spirit—slipped out of the top

of the reliquary. More began to follow, disappearing into puffs of smoke as they reached toward Anya.

Somehow they knew that the one remaining Romanov was near.

"Oh come on now," said Bartok. "Am I supposed to believe this thing woke up after all these years just because some guy claims she's a Romanov?"

The reliquary glowed brightly, and began to shake.

Bartok was frightened. "Okay! Okay!" he said. "I get the message! Enough already with the smoke, people."

He took another look at Anya, far below.

"If that thing's come back to life," he mused, "it must mean Anastasia's alive and that's her."

Suddenly the reliquary shot off like a rocket, dragging the white bat with it. Bartok covered his eyes as they crashed through the floor, down into the icy waters of a lake, down, down, down . . .

"Helllllllp!" Bartok hollered.

At last he landed in a strange cavelike chamber far beneath the surface of the earth.

As he peeked out of the rubble, he saw someone he knew.

Or *used* to know.

Rasputin!

But he was supposed to be dead! Bartok had seen him drown with his own eyes. And yet here was his rotting corpse up and walking around.

"Bartok?" Rasputin gasped.

"Oh, master, is that you?"

"Yeah, in a manner of speaking . . ." Rasputin shrugged, and his eyeball dropped out of his withered face.

Plop! Bartok caught it.

Bartok's stomach lurched. "Whoa, that fell right out of there, sir." He tossed the eyeball back like a hot potato.

"Something's happened," Rasputin growled as he screwed the eyeball back in place. "I knew it! I could feel the dark forces stirring! What is it? Tell me!"

Bartok told how he'd seen Anastasia at the old palace.

"Anastasia? Alive!" Rasputin frowned and his lips fell off.

Bartok couldn't take his eyes off them. "Uh, sir, your lips . . . ?"

Rasputin grabbed Bartok. "That Romanov brat. *That's* why I'm stuck here in limbo! My curse is unfulfilled!"

Woefully, he flung out his arms. The hand holding Bartok flew off and smacked into the wall.

Rasputin groaned. "Look at me, Bartok. I'm falling apart. I'm a wreck!"

Bartok carried the hand back to his master. "Actually, sir, considering how long you've been dead, you look pretty good."

Rasputin began to cry.

"Sir, you do, you do!" Bartok insisted.

Rasputin looked up hopefully. "Really?"

"Sir, is this the face of a bat who would lie to you?"

Rasputin sighed. "If only I hadn't lost the gift from the dark forces, the key to my powers."

Bartok smiled. Time to score points with the boss! He picked up the reliquary from the rubble. "What? You mean this?"

Rasputin's eyes popped open. "Oh, where did you get that? Give it to me!" He snatched it from Bartok's hands and laughed.

He had once been the most powerful mystical man in Russia. Now he was a card-carrying member of the walking dead. And that blasted Romanov family was to blame. But now he would have his revenge!

Rasputin stroked the reliquary. "My old friend. Together again," he said, and laughed. "Now my dark purpose will be fulfilled, and the last of the Romanovs will die!"

Chapter Three

The train chugged steadily across the snowy Russian countryside.

Who cares that our compartment is old and worn? Anya thought. *It's taking us to Paris!*

Vladimir tickled Pooka with his feathered quill, then dipped it in a bottle of black ink. Anya didn't know it, but he was busy drawing up their fake travel papers.

Dimitri stowed their luggage overhead, then sat down.

Growl!

He stood up quickly. He'd nearly sat on Pooka!

The dog growled again.

Dimitri growled back!

Then he sneezed and sat down next to Anya. "The mutt gets the window seat, does he?"

But Anya only shrugged. She stared out the window, playing with her necklace.

"Stop fiddling with that thing!" Dimitri ordered. "And sit up straight. Remember, you're a grand duchess."

Anya glared over her shoulder. "How is it that you know what grand duchesses do or don't do?"

"I make it my business to know," he snapped back. Then he rubbed his face with his hands. What was he doing, bickering with this girl? He needed to control his temper to keep his plan on track. He needed her to believe he was only trying to help her find her family. The reward money depended on it!

"Look," he added more gently. "I'm just trying to help. All right?"

Across the car, Vladimir rolled his eyes.

Anya didn't like getting ordered around—whether by fat, balding headmistresses or handsome young men. "Dimitri," she said, her voice as sweet as honey. "Do you *really* think I'm royalty?"

"You know I do," Dimitri answered seriously.

"Then stop bossing me around!" She stuck her

tongue out at him. Dimitri made a face.

"Well," Vladimir said with a hearty laugh. "She certainly has a mind of her own!"

◉

Later that afternoon, Anya pretended to be reading a book when Dimitri came in.

"Look," he said, "I think we got off on the wrong foot."

Anya put her book down and looked right at Dimitri. "Well, I think we did, too. But I appreciate your apology."

"Apology!" Dimitri exclaimed. "Who said anything about an apology? I was just saying—"

"Oh, don't talk to me anymore, okay?" Anya said, her face flushed with anger. "It's only going to upset me."

"Fine. I'll be quiet, if you will."

"Fine."

"Fine!"

Anya stared out the window. As she watched her homeland race past, she felt as if she were leaving a piece of her heart behind. "Do you think you're going to miss it?" she murmured.

"Miss what?" Dimitri asked. "Your talking?"

"No! Russia!"

Dimitri chuckled and shook his head. "Nope!"

"But it was your home," Anya said.

"It was a place where I once lived. End of story."

"Well, then," Anya went on, "you must plan on making Paris your home."

Dimitri shook his head, exasperated. "What is it with you and homes?"

"Well, for one thing, a home is something that every *normal* person wants," Anya replied crossly. "And for another thing, it's a place where you . . ."

"What?"

"You know," Anya began. But his big brown-eyed stare made her tongue-tied. "Oh, just forget it . . ."

Just then Vladimir came into the car, whistling. He had Pooka cradled in his arms.

"Thank goodness it's you!" Anya exclaimed, jumping to her feet. She pointed a finger at Dimitri and ordered, "Please remove him from my sight!"

Pooka began barking.

"What have you done to her?" Vladimir asked.

"Me?" Dimitri exclaimed, amazed. "It's her!"

"Ha!" Anya spun around and stomped out the door.

SLAM!

Vladimir chuckled and lifted the barking Pooka into the air. "Oh, no. An unspoken attraction!"

"Attraction!" Dimitri exclaimed. "To that skinny little brat? Have you lost your mind?"

Then Dimitri stormed out, too.

SLAM!

Vladimir laughed out loud. "Like two peas in a pod!"

❀

Night descended like a black velvet curtain. Snow clouds blocked out the moon and stars. There was not even a farmhouse in sight. The darkness seemed to stretch to the ends of the earth.

Suddenly, an explosion ripped through the night. Something crashed through the brittle limbs of winter trees. Eerie flames streaked across the darkness like comets.

Rasputin's minions had come for the Romanov princess.

As ugly as gargoyles, with batlike wings, the tiny demons crawled over the train's engine like maggots. They poked and prodded and yanked at the controls.

The engine sped up, faster and faster, glowing hot and red against the frozen white snow.

The minions cackled with glee.

❀

Vladimir had gone to brush his teeth. Now he made his way down the narrow aisle of the train. As he squeezed around a couple, their words stopped him in his tracks.

"Last month the traveling papers were in blue,"

the man said. "But now they're red."

Vladimir gasped and peered over the man's shoulder at the papers. Sure enough, theirs were written in red ink.

Quickly he reached into his pocket for his own traveling papers. The ones they needed in order to leave the country.

He'd written them in black ink. The guards would know at a glance that these were fake.

"Papers!" a guard called out down the aisle.

Oh, no! Vladimir raced back to his compartment. Anya was already curled up in her bunk, sound asleep. He hurriedly explained to Dimitri that their papers were no good.

"I propose we move to the baggage car," Vladimir said. "Quickly, before the guards come!"

Dimitri shook Anya to wake her up.

WHAM! She slugged him.

Dimitri fell back into the seat, holding his nose. "Hey!"

Anya woke up, startled. "Oh, it's you. Sorry."

Dimitri picked up the luggage, then grabbed Anya's hand and pulled her toward the door. "Come on, we've got to go."

"Where are we going?" she demanded sleepily.

"I think you broke my nose," was the reply.

Anya just shook her head and pulled on her coat

as she followed him down the aisle.

The baggage car was near the front of the train.

"Ah, yes," Dimitri whispered as he closed the door behind them. "This will do nicely."

Vladimir shivered. "She'll freeze in here."

"She can thaw in Paris," Dimitri shot back.

Anya looked around. The baggage car was a cold, dark jumble of boxes, bags, and crates. Not exactly royal accommodations.

It was the kind of place somebody would hide out in.

"The baggage car?" She crossed her arms and tapped her foot. "There wouldn't be anything wrong with our papers, would there?"

"Of course not, Your Grace," Dimitri assured her. "It's just that, uh, I hate to see you forced to mingle with all those commoners."

Anya opened her mouth to reply when—

KABOOM!

Beneath them, the minions blew apart the coupling that connected the baggage car to the rest of the train.

Anya and her friends were thrown to the floor.

"What was that?" Dimitri said from beneath a pile of luggage.

Vladimir peered out the window of the car's back door. "I don't know, but there goes the dining car."

They were leaving the rest of the train behind.

But that wasn't the worst of it. Vladimir pointed out the window to the locomotive.

The engine was blowing smoke and fire.

Dimitri struggled to his feet. "Something's not right. Wait here, I'll check it out."

When Dimitri reached the locomotive he had to shield his face from the heat. Where was the engineer? "Hello! Anybody here?"

No one answered.

Maybe he could stop the train himself. He grabbed a lever—*ouch!*—and burned his hand. Green fire exploded upward. Gasping in surprise, he scrambled back to the baggage car, dirty and singed.

"We're going way too fast!" Anya cried.

"Nobody's driving this train," Dimitri explained. "It's out of control. We're going to have to jump!"

Anya's eyebrow shot up. "After you."

She pointed toward the window.

The train was roaring around the side of a steep mountain. They squinted into the darkness and looked down a sheer cliff.

To jump would mean certain death.

What would they do?

Chapter Four

"Okay." Dimitri ran his hands through his hair, thinking fast. "We'll unhook the baggage car from the engine."

It was worth a try.

Dimitri crawled out between the two cars. An icy wind whipped through his clothes as he struggled to unhook their car from the speeding engine.

He struck the latch with a hammer, but *BANG!* the hammer broke!

That was strange. It was almost as if something— or someone—had welded the couplings together. As if they wanted to make sure the cars couldn't be separated.

Anya and Vladimir searched through the baggage for something else Dimitri could use. Pooka barked at a box. Anya knelt down to read the label: DANGER! EXPLOSIVES.

She grinned.

"Come on!" Dimitri shouted into the wind. "There's got to be something in there better than this!"

Seconds later Anya handed him a lighted stick of dynamite.

He glanced back at her, impressed. Pretty fast work for a princess! "That'll do."

He shoved the hissing stick of dynamite into the coupling. "Go, go, go!" he shouted to the others as he hustled them to the back of the car. They huddled behind a steamer trunk and waited.

"What do they teach you in those orphanages, anyway?" he asked Anya.

BOOM!

The dynamite exploded, showering them with scraps of metal and bits of wood. The whole front end of the car was blown away.

But they were all fine, and the engine was pulling away in front of them. They were free!

Rasputin's minions howled in rage. They raced ahead of the engine, toward a bridge in the distance.

Meanwhile, Vladimir strained to turn the huge wheel that controlled the baggage car's brakes. But the wheel broke off in his hands.

"Don't worry," Dimitri said. "We've got plenty of track. We'll just coast to a stop."

But the car began to pick up speed as they headed downhill toward the bridge—the bridge that the minions had just blown to pieces! It erupted in green fire. Pieces of it spewed high into the air. The minions were delighted. The runaway engine was headed straight for the edge.

The baggage car would be next!

"You were saying?" Anya asked.

Thinking quickly, Dimitri grabbed a chain that was wrapped around some freight boxes. "I've got an idea. Vlad, give me a hand with this."

Dimitri edged his way out of the car. As the ground whizzed by beneath him, he lowered himself under the carriage. "Vlad, hand me the chain!" he yelled.

But Dimitri hadn't noticed that Vladimir had lost his balance, falling into a box.

He was stunned to see Anya hanging out of the car, holding the chain toward him. "Not you!"

Anya grinned. "Vladimir's busy at the moment."

Dimitri took the chain and wrapped it around the

steel beam of the undercarriage.

Just then a shower of twisted steel from the front of the car flew back at him like shrapnel.

With Anya's help he yanked himself up just as the steel whizzed by, shattering a tree.

"That could have been you," Anya whispered.

"If we live through this," Dimitri gasped, "remind me to thank you."

But there was no time to waste now. The baggage car was speeding toward the gorge.

Dimitri jumped to his feet. "Here goes nothing. Brace yourself!" The other end of the chain had a metal hook which he flung out the back. If the hook caught on the tracks, it would stop them like a ship's anchor.

Instead it bounced.

And bounced again.

And another time.

Anya looked out the front of the car. They were almost at the bridge!

Finally the hook caught on one of the wooden railroad ties. It tore through the tie, caught another, and ripped through again. The third one stuck and yanked the chain tight.

The floor of the baggage car ripped from the wheels and turned sideways on the track, plowing

Marie gives her youngest granddaughter a beautiful music box to remember her by.

An angry Rasputin casts a curse on the Romanov family.

Which way should Anya go? Maybe Pooka can help!

Dimitri and Vladimir begin the plot to find an Anastasia look-alike.

The eyes, the hands! The resemblance is startling!

Dimitri, Vladimir, and Pooka teach Anya how to be a princess.

Could it be love?

Dimitri rescues Anya from Rasputin's evil spell.

Shocked, Dimitri realizes that Anya really is Anastasia Romanov.

Anya and Dimitri at the Russian Ballet nervously waiting to meet with Marie.

A furious Anya discovers that she was part of Dimitri's con game!

"Anastasia! My Anastasia!" Together in Paris at last.

The topiary garden has come to life!

Rasputin is attacked by his own minions.

The fight is finally over—but did it cost Dimitri his life?

Anastasia and Dimitri—a new beginning.

through the snow like a runaway sled.

"Well, this is our stop," Anya called out.

The four leaped out of the car . . .

. . . and landed in a snowdrift.

They watched as the engine plunged over the broken bridge. Seconds later, it exploded in a fireball at the bottom of the gorge.

Vladimir lay in the snow, holding the whimpering Pooka in his arms. "Is everyone okay?" he asked.

"I'm fine," Anya said.

"Her Grace is fine," Dimitri grumbled. "I may never walk again, but she's fine." He stood up, checking for broken bones. "I hate trains. Remind me never to get on a train again."

❁

"Nooooo!" Deep in the earth Rasputin screamed in agony.

"Wow, take it easy there," Bartok warned him. "Think of your blood pressure!"

Rasputin had watched every moment of the train wreck through the images in his reliquary. "How could they let her escape?"

"You're right," Bartok said. "It's very upsetting, sir." He picked up the small reliquary. "I guess this thing's broken." With a sigh, he tossed it over his shoulder.

Rasputin's dark eyes widened in terror. "You idiot!" he screamed. He leaped through the air to catch it.

But he knew he'd never make it. So he flung his hand off, and it skidded across the floor.

The reliquary landed safely in the palm of his disconnected hand.

Rasputin gasped in relief. Then he turned his fiery red gaze on Bartok.

"All right, sir," Bartok said, backing away. "Take it easy. Just remember what I said about stress . . ."

Rasputin shoved the reliquary up against Bartok's tiny nose. "I sold my soul for this. My life, my very existence depends on it, and you almost destroyed it!"

Bartok tried to squirm away. "I get it! I get it! You break it, you bought it," he said.

"See that you remember, you miserable rodent," Rasputin snarled.

"Oh, sure, blame the bat," Bartok mumbled. "What the heck. We're easy targets."

Rasputin shot him a dirty look. "What are you muttering about?"

"Uh, Anastasia, sir," Bartok said quickly. "Just wishing I could do the job for you." He made a few karate chops in the air. "Hi-ya!" he said, tripping and falling onto the floor.

Rasputin shook his head, disgusted. Then his thoughts returned to the girl. He could not rest until the very last Romanov was destroyed. "I have something else in mind. Something more enticing. Something really cruel . . ."

It would take weeks for Dimitri's party to cross the mountains into Europe. Rasputin had plenty of time.

Chapter Five

By the time Anya and her friends descended from the mountains, flowers peeked through the melting patches of snow. The sun shone brightly. Spring was in the air.

"Sophie, my dear, Vlady's on his way!" the old aristocrat shouted.

Oops! Dimitri wished his friend hadn't mentioned Sophie yet.

"Who's Sophie?" Anya asked.

"Who's Sophie!" Vladimir exclaimed. A strange look crossed his face. It was either indigestion—or love.

"She's a tender little morsel. The cup of hot chocolate after a long walk in the snow. She's a pastry filled with whipped cream and laughter! She's—"

"Is this a person or a cream puff?" Anya asked dryly.

Vladimir sighed and began to pick flowers. "She is the Empress's charming first cousin."

"What!" Anya exclaimed. "But I thought we were going to see the Empress herself. Why are we going to see her cousin?"

Dimitri shrugged. They had sort of forgotten to tell her . . . on purpose. "Well, nobody gets near the Empress Marie without convincing Sophie first."

"Oh, no." Anya shook her head. "Not me, no. Nobody ever told me I had to *prove* I was the Grand Duchess. Show up, yes. Look nice, fine. But lie?" She fiddled nervously with her necklace.

Dimitri tried to calm her down. "You don't know it's a lie. What if it's true? Okay, so there's one more stop on the road to finding out who you are. I just thought this was something you had to see through to the end. No matter what."

"But look at me!" Anya wailed. "I'm not exactly Grand Duchess material here." She stomped off down the hill, too angry to talk about it.

Dimitri started to follow her, but Vladimir held him back. Instead the old count followed her down the hillside. He joined her on a bridge, where she stood staring into the stream.

Vladimir gestured toward the water below. "Tell me, child. What do you see?"

Anya gazed at her reflection in the slow-moving water. Her face was smudged. Her mop of bright red hair was a mess. Her boyish hand-me-down clothes were dirty and torn. "I see a skinny little nobody," she muttered, "with no past and no future."

Vladimir laughed softly and took her hand. "I see an engaging and fiery young woman. Who on a number of occasions has shown a regal command equal to any royalty in the world." He chuckled. "And I have known my share of royalty."

Anya sighed, studying her reflection. Could there really be a princess hiding beneath the torn clothes and dirty face? It didn't seem possible.

Then Dimitri's face appeared next to hers, reflected in the sparkling waters.

"So," he said cheerfully. "Are you ready to become the Grand Duchess Anastasia?"

Anya bristled. She was still mad at him for not telling her about this Sophie person.

Vladimir shot him a look.

"What?" Dimitri asked, confused.

Vladimir gestured to him to keep his mouth shut,

just for a moment longer. If they weren't careful, their "Anastasia" just might go running back to the orphanage.

"There's nothing left for you back there, you know," he said gently. "Everything is in Paris."

Anya's hand went to her necklace. *"Together in Paris,"* she said softly.

Maybe she wasn't the real Anastasia. But whoever she was, the answers to all her questions lay in Paris.

And this was her only chance to get there.

With a shake of her head, Anya stood up straight and pounded her fist on the railing. "Gentlemen . . ."

They looked at her anxiously.

Anya grinned. "Start your teaching!"

Her comrades cheered and linked arms with her as they headed down the road.

"You were born in a palace by the sea," Dimitri began.

"You rode horseback when you were only three," Vladimir added.

And that was only the beginning.

They made her memorize the names of all her royal relatives. How to stand up straight and curtsy just so. There was so much to learn, and so little time.

Paris was only days away!

"Hey, what do you have there?" Anya asked Dimitri the next day. They were standing in the hallway of the ship that would take them to Paris.

Dimitri shrugged. "I bought you a dress."

Anya held it up and frowned. It was several sizes too large. "You bought me a *tent!*"

Dimitri didn't laugh. "Come on, just put it on." He left the cabin in a huff.

As soon as he was gone, Anya held up the dress and twirled around the hallway. "A dress . . . hmm!" Of course, it needed a lot of work. But she couldn't remember when she'd had a new dress of her very own. Especially one so beautiful! But she'd never let Dimitri know how happy he'd made her.

❁

At sunset Dimitri and Vladimir sat on the deck playing chess. Dimitri glanced up as a beautiful girl strolled out onto the deck. Then he did a double take.

It was Anya!

He could hardly believe his eyes. The skinny little spitfire of a tomboy had somehow transformed into an elegant princess!

Vladimir pulled himself to his feet, beaming at their creation. "Wonderful! Marvelous!" he exclaimed. "And now that you are dressed for a ball, you will learn to dance at one." He snapped his fingers. "Dimitri!"

Dimitri held up his hands. "I'm not very good at it."

But Vladimir insisted. Anya put out her arms to dance. As music drifted out from the ship's ballroom, Dimitri took her in his arms.

"And one-two-three, one-two-three . . ." Vladimir counted out the waltz. "No, no, Anya. *You* don't lead. Let *him!*"

They danced in silence for a few minutes. Dimitri nervously cleared his throat. "That dress really is beautiful."

"Do you think so?" Anya asked.

"Yes. I mean, it was nice on the hanger, but it looks even better on you. You should wear it."

Anya giggled. "I *am* wearing it."

"Right, of course. I'm just trying to give you a . . ."

"Compliment?" Anya suggested.

"Yes, of course."

Anya smiled as they swirled across the deck. Little by little, their awkward steps blossomed into a graceful dance.

"I'm feeling a little dizzy," Anya said at last.

"Me too," Dimitri said. "Probably from the spinning."

Their steps slowed, but Dimitri still held her in his arms.

"Maybe we should stop," he said.

"We *have* stopped," Anya pointed out.

Suddenly, Vladimir saw something he hadn't seen before. And yet it was as plain as the mustache on his face.

Anya and Dimitri were falling in love!

Chapter Six

That night the ship tossed and turned.

Vladimir groaned. His face was a bit green.

"Are you all right?" Anya whispered. They had settled down for the night. But a storm was keeping her and Vladimir awake.

"Fine, fine," Vladimir sighed. "Just full of envy. Look at him!" He jerked a thumb at Dimitri curled up, sound asleep on the floor. "He can sleep through anything!"

Pooka climbed up on Dimitri's backpack. The ship tilted, and the little dog tumbled off, knocking the backpack over.

A little jeweled box tumbled out of the pack. Curious, Anya picked it up.

A shiver ran through her.

"Pretty jewelry box, isn't it?" Vladimir asked.

Anya shook her head. "Are you sure that's what it is?"

"What else could it be?"

"Something else," Anya said softly. "Something special. Something to do with a secret." She laughed. "Is that possible?"

Vladimir climbed into his bunk. "Anything's possible. You taught Dimitri how to waltz, didn't you?" Vladimir yawned. "Sleep well, Your Majesty."

Anya smiled and tucked the tiny box back into Dimitri's pack. Then she crawled into her own bunk with Pooka snuggled up beside her. "Sweet dreams, Pooka," she whispered.

❁

Rasputin peered into his reliquary and watched Anya's eyelids flutter closed.

"There she is, master," Bartok whispered. "Sound asleep in her little bed."

Smoky images swirled around the reliquary. Faces, trees, a lake . . . Rasputin chuckled with delight. With a puff of his rotten breath, he blew the cloud of images into the air, then whispered,

"Pleasant dreams, Princess."

❀

Out at sea the ship pitched in the storm. But at last all was quiet. Even the seasick Vladimir had managed to fall asleep.

Smoky images slithered under the cabin door.

They flowed over Dimitri. They swirled across the floor. They flowed up into the bunk where Anya lay sleeping.

The smoke hovered a moment, waiting.

Anya yawned.

The smoky images darted into her mouth. Images of butterflies fluttered around her eyes.

Anya smiled as Rasputin's dream began . . .

❀

She woke up in a beautiful meadow. Her little brother waved to her. Large butterflies filled the air.

Anya rose from her bed, her eyes closed. Walking softly in her sleep, she slipped out the cabin door. It closed behind her.

Anya followed her brother. The butterflies flew around her head. She climbed a hill covered with daffodils. In the distance she saw her three sisters on top of a huge rock. They waved to her, then dived into a sparkling mountain pool.

Back in the cabin Pooka woke up just as Anya left.

He scratched at the closed door, but couldn't get out. So he ran to Dimitri and barked in his ear.

At first Dimitri just rolled over and pulled a blanket over his head. But at last he struggled awake. "What, Pooka?"

Pooka jumped up onto Anya's bed and barked.

The bed was empty.

Dimitri was on his feet in an instant. He dashed out the cabin door and searched the darkness for any sign of her. Sea spray drenched him as the storm battered the ship. "Anya!" he shouted. He didn't see her anywhere!

Splash! Anya watched her little brother dive into the pool. It looked like so much fun! Her family waved at her and called for her to join them.

Anya smiled and grabbed a thick hanging vine.

Dimitri climbed the ship's ladder two steps at a time. As he reached the upper deck, the restless sea crashed over him and swept him up into the crow's nest. Wiping the seawater from his eyes, he searched the deck for a glimpse of Anya.

Suddenly he spotted her.

"Anya! No!" he shouted.

She stood on the railing of the deck. She was holding on to a long thick rope.

And she was about to jump to her death!

Chapter Seven

Anya was still dreaming.

Her father waved to her. "Join us," he said. "Jump in!"

Anya nodded. She held tight to the rope. But just as she was about to jump, her father's face changed. His handsome features twisted into a dark and frightening face. An evil face.

The face of Rasputin!

His minions swirled around her, poking and prodding.

"Jump!" Rasputin cried. "The Romanov curse. JUMP!"

Someone grabbed her around the waist.

She was falling!

"Anya! Anya, wake up!"

Anya jolted awake.

She was in Dimitri's arms. He'd swooped down on a rope and rescued her from diving into the stormy sea.

Anya cried out when she saw what she'd almost done. Shaking, she clung to Dimitri. "The Romanov curse!" she cried.

Dimitri searched her face. "What are you talking about?"

"I keep seeing faces," Anya gasped. "So many faces." Then she began to cry.

Dimitri held her close. "It was a nightmare," he said softly. "It's all right. You're safe now."

But was she?

❖

"No! Not again!" Rasputin moaned and clutched his head in frustration, and his fingers sank into his rotten skull.

"Easy, master," Bartok said. "This is no time to lose your head."

With effort, Rasputin calmed down. "You're right." He took a deep breath. "I am calm. I am heartless. I have no feelings."

Another deep breath, and he opened his eyes, suddenly smiling. "I feel a sudden onset of clear thinking. I'll just have to kill her myself. In person."

"Ugh!" Bartok exclaimed. "What, you mean—physically?"

"You know what they say," Rasputin said. "If you want something done right . . ."

"But that means—going topside?"

"Exactly." Rasputin checked himself over to make sure all his parts were properly attached. "I have so many fond memories of Paris. Killing the last of the Romanovs will be so delicious. Well, time to go."

"But you're dead!" Bartok shrieked. "You're falling apart! Sir, excuse me, but how do you expect to get to Paris in one piece?"

Rasputin laughed. "I thought we'd take the train."

He raised his reliquary. Thunder rumbled through the earthen walls of his cave. Lightning flashed. Smoke billowed through the room as he rocketed through the ceiling.

Next stop—Paris, France.

Chapter Eight

The young woman sat on the edge of her chair. The two women staring at her in the fancy drawing room made her nervous. But she held her head high. Like a princess.

"Ah, yes, I remember so well," she said. "Uncle Yashin was from Moscow. Uncle Boris was from Odessa. And every spring—"

"We would take picnics by the shore on Sunday," another voice finished. The Dowager Empress Marie leaned forward and frowned at the girl. "Haven't you anything better to do?"

The young woman sputtered with indignation as

Marie's plump cousin Sophie swept her out the door. "Oh, dear, you have to leave now? Good-bye." She closed the door firmly in her face.

Sophie bustled back to Marie's side and poured her a cup of tea. "Oh, I must say I'm sorry. I thought that one was surely real." She set a cup of tea in front of her cat Tilly. The cat sniffed and turned up her nose.

Sophie clucked her tongue, and plopped another lump of sugar into the cat's tea. The cat purred and began to drink.

"But we won't be fooled next time!" Sophie insisted. "I'm going to think of some really hard questions—"

"No," Marie interrupted. "My heart can't take it anymore!" She gazed sadly at a photograph of Anastasia. Then she placed it facedown on the desk.

"I will see no more girls claiming to be Anastasia!"

❖

Anya trembled as she stood on the steps of Sophie's townhouse that afternoon. What was she *doing* here? She felt like gathering the skirts of her new dress and running off in the opposite direction.

Smiling, Vladimir knocked.

A maid opened the door. "*Oui, Monsieur?*" she said. Sophie came to the door and gasped with delight at what she saw.

Vladimir threw his arms open wide. "Sophie Stanislovskievna Somorkov-Smirnoff!"

Sophie's eyes lit up. Her jaw dropped in amazement. "Vladimir Vanya Voinitsky Vasilovich! Well, this is unexpected. Come in! Come in, everyone!"

Bubbling with excitement, Sophie led her guests into her elegant drawing room. How wonderful to meet an old friend from Russia! Especially one as dashing as Vladimir Vasilovich!

But Vladimir had one more surprise. With a sweeping bow, he announced, "May I present her Imperial Highness, the Grand Duchess Anastasia Nikolayevna!"

Anya blushed and offered her best curtsy.

"Oh, my heavens!" Sophie gasped. "She certainly does look like Anastasia." Then she sighed. "But so did many of the others."

When everyone was seated, Sophie began her questions: names, places, dates, times.

Anya answered them all.

At last Sophie leaned back in her chair. She'd asked her the toughest questions. Yet this young girl had answered each one without hesitation. Was she a clever actress? Or could she really be the girl they'd been searching for?

"Finally, you may find this an impertinent question,

but indulge me," Sophie said. "How did you escape during the siege of the palace?"

Dimitri and Vladimir exchanged nervous glances. That was one question they hadn't practiced with Anya. Would she be quick enough to fake an acceptable answer?

Anya blinked. She was silent for a moment, her mind a blank. Then her mind snagged a wisp of a memory. "There was a boy . . ." she began. "A boy who worked in the palace. He opened the wall—" She shook her head, her cheeks hot from embarrassment. "I'm sorry, that's crazy! Walls opening . . ."

The others laughed.

But not Dimitri. He rose to his feet, staring at Anya as if he'd never seen her before.

It was not possible!

Dimitri had been that boy at the palace. He was the one who had opened the wall—the secret passage—to help the Romanovs escape. Only two other people had been there. The Dowager Empress Marie and her granddaughter Anastasia.

How could Anya possibly know about that night? Unless . . .

. . . Anya really was Anastasia!

Dimitri quickly excused himself and hurried into the garden. He needed to think.

"So," Vladimir asked Sophie. "Is she a Romanov?"

"Well," Sophie said, "she answered every question . . ."

Anya's face lit up.

"You hear that, child?" Vladimir exclaimed. "You did it!" He and Anya hugged.

"So," Vladimir said, "when do we go and see the Empress?"

Sophie cleared her throat and glanced away. "I'm afraid you don't. The Empress won't see any more girls."

"What!" Vladimir exclaimed. "Now, Sophie, my bright diamond. Surely you can think of some way to arrange a brief interview." He crossed his arms and leaned back in his chair. "I refuse to budge till you think of something. Please?"

Sophie thought for a moment. Then she grinned. "Do you like the Russian Ballet? I believe they're performing in Paris tonight." She winked. "The Dowager Empress and I *love* the Russian Ballet. We *never* miss it."

That was it! They'd see the Empress at the ballet!

Chapter Nine

That night a very nervous Vladimir paced the steps of the Paris Opera House.

Dimitri sat on the steps with his head in his hands. "We don't have anything to be nervous about," he told his friend. "She's the Princess—"

"I know," Vladimir said, wringing his hands. "But—"

"No, no, no, you *don't* know," Dimitri insisted. He grabbed his friend by the shoulders and looked him in the eye. "I was the boy in the palace. The one who opened the wall."

The old aristocrat frowned, confused.

"She's the real thing, Vlad," Dimitri said softly.

Vladimir's jaw dropped. "That means our Anya has found her family!" he exclaimed happily. "We have found the heir to the Russian throne! And you . . ."

When he saw his friend's face, his smile faded.

"I'll walk out of her life forever," Dimitri finished.

"But—"

Dimitri shook his head. "We're going to go through with this as if nothing has changed."

Vladimir frowned. "You've got to tell her."

"Tell me what?" Anya said, suddenly appearing at Dimitri's side.

Dimitri gazed at their little orphan. She had never looked lovelier—or more like a princess. "How beautiful you look," he said. Then he took her arm and led her up the stairs to their seats in the balcony.

Anya was so nervous she barely watched the dancers. She tore up her program into tiny pieces.

Dimitri reached over and took her hand. "Everything's going to be fine," he said with a smile.

But inside, he knew it wasn't going to be fine. At least not for him.

When the lights came up for intermission, Dimitri sadly took her hand. "Come on. I guess it's time."

Together the three friends made their way to the

Empress's private balcony.

"Wait here," Dimitri whispered. "I'll go in and announce you properly."

Anya laid a gloved hand on his arm. "Dimitri—"

"Yes?"

She took a deep breath. "Look, we've been through a lot together. And I just wanted to . . ."

"Yes?"

Anya fidgeted with a ribbon on her gown. "Well, thank you, I guess. Yes, thank you for everything."

Dimitri smiled, but his eyes were sad. "Good luck, I guess," he replied. Then he entered the Empress's private balcony.

Sophie sneaked him a wink.

Dimitri bowed crisply. "Please inform Her Majesty, the Dowager Empress, that I have found her granddaughter, the Grand Duchess Anastasia. She's waiting to see her just outside the door."

Marie turned in her seat, her face filled with anger. "You may tell that rude young man that I have seen enough Grand Duchess Anastasias to last me a lifetime! Now if you'll excuse me, I wish to live out the remainder of my lonely life in peace."

"Your Majesty," Dimitri said. "My name is Dimitri. I used to work in the palace."

"Well, that's one I haven't heard," Marie said

dryly as she stood to leave.

"Wait!" Dimitri begged. "Don't go, please. If you'll just hear me out."

The old woman's blue eyes burned with rage. "I know what you're after. I've seen it before! Men who train young women in the royal ways."

"But if Your Highness will—"

"Haven't you been listening?" Marie cried. "I've had enough. I don't care how much you have fashioned this girl to look like her. Or sound like her. Or act like her. In the end, it never is her!"

"This time it *is* her!" Dimitri said.

Marie stepped back, her eyes narrowed. "Dimitri . . . I've heard of you. You're that con man from St. Petersburg who was holding auditions to find an Anastasia look-alike!"

"It's not what you think," Dimitri said.

"How much pain will you inflict on an old woman for ten million rubles?" The Empress called the guards. "Remove him at once!"

"But she is Anastasia!" Dimitri insisted. "If you'll only speak to her, you'll see!"

The guards threw him from the box, and he landed at Anya's feet. When his eyes met hers, he knew she'd heard everything.

"It was all a lie, wasn't it?" she whispered. "You

used me. I was just a part of your con game to get her money!"

"No," Dimitri insisted, taking her by the hands. "Look, it may have started out that way. But everything's different now. Because you're Anastasia. You really are!"

"Stop it!" Anya cried. "You lied from the beginning. And I not only believed you, I-I actually . . ."

"Anya, please," Dimitri persisted. "When you spoke of the hidden door in the wall, and the boy—listen to me, that was—"

"NO!" Anya cried, pulling away from him. "Just leave me alone." She slapped him, then ran for the stairs.

"Anya, please!" Dimitri called after her. "You have to know the truth!"

By the time he reached the front steps of the Paris Opera House, Anya had disappeared into the crowd.

Then he spotted the Dowager Empress coming down the steps. Her driver helped her into her car. That gave him an idea.

Moments later, Marie's car roared off into the night.

"Ilya, slow down!" Marie ordered her driver.

The driver glanced back over his shoulder. "I'm not Ilya, and I won't slow down. Not until you listen."

Marie stared at Dimitri, her mouth open in shock. "You! How dare you! Stop this car immediately!"

But Dimitri didn't stop until he pulled up in front of Sophie's townhouse. He jumped from the car and ran around to open Marie's door.

"You have to talk to her," he insisted. "Just look at her. *Please!*"

Marie tried to shove past him. But then Dimitri pulled something from his pocket. "Do you recognize this?"

Marie froze as he thrust the tiny jeweled box into her hands. She'd know that box anywhere.

It was the one she'd given Anastasia the night she disappeared.

"Where did you get this?" she demanded, her voice nearly a whisper.

"I know you've been hurt," Dimitri said softly. "But it's just possible that she's been as lost and alone as you."

Marie raised an eyebrow. "You'll stop at nothing, will you?"

Dimitri shrugged. "I'm probably almost as stubborn as you are."

Clutching the music box to her chest, Marie walked to the door.

❖

Inside Sophie's house, Anya was packing. She wasn't sure where she was going. But she had to get away. Tonight!

There was a knock at the door.

"Go away, Dimitri!" she called out angrily.

Slowly, the door creaked open. Anya turned and gasped.

The Dowager Empress Marie stood in the doorway.

"Oh," Anya gasped, "I thought you were—"

"I know very well who you thought I was," Marie said sharply. "The question is, who exactly are *you?*"

Anya gulped. "I . . . I was hoping you could tell me."

The Empress sighed and perched on the edge of a chair. "My dear, I'm old and tired of being conned and tricked."

"I don't want to trick you," Anya insisted.

"And I suppose the money doesn't interest you, either?"

"I just want to know who I am," Anya replied. "Whether or not I belong to a family. Your family."

Marie stood abruptly, her face a tight mask. "You're a very good actress. The best yet, in fact. But I've had enough." She swept past Anya toward the door.

Anya sniffed the air. "Peppermint . . ."

Marie froze, her hand on the doorknob. She shrugged. "An oil for my hands."

Anya's eyes drifted closed as the fragrance brought back a rush of memories. "Yes . . . I spilled a bottle. The carpet was soaked. And it forever smelled of peppermint." She opened her eyes. "Like you!"

Marie could only stare as Anya continued.

"I used to lie on that rug, and oh, how I missed you when you went away. When you came here. To Paris."

Only then did Marie notice Anya fiddling with her necklace. A necklace that held a flower-shaped key.

"What is that?" she asked, afraid that she knew.

"This?" Anya held it up. "Well, I've always had it. Ever since before I can remember."

Marie crossed the room to Anya's side and held out her hand. "May I?"

Puzzled, Anya gave her the key.

Marie removed the jeweled music box from her evening bag and showed it to Anya. As her blue eyes filled with tears, Marie whispered, "It was our secret. My Anastasia's and mine."

Anya reached for the key. Somehow she knew how to fit the key to the box to wind it. "The music box . . . to sing me to sleep when you were in Paris . . ."

Anya hummed the melody that had haunted her for years. Seconds later, the music box echoed her song.

Tears streamed down Marie's wrinkled cheeks as she joined Anya in the lullaby:

"Hear this song and remember,
Soon you'll be home with me
Once upon a December . . ."

Their voices ended in a whisper.

Their search was over.

"Anastasia!" Marie gasped. "My Anastasia!"

Then they hugged each other as if they would never let go.

Dimitri stood on the street, gazing up at Anastasia's window. Then he blew a kiss and walked away.

Chapter Ten

The next day Dimitri stood before the Dowager Empress in her study. "You sent for me, Your Grace?"

Marie nodded toward a small suitcase filled with the reward money. "Ten million rubles. As promised. With my gratitude."

"I accept your gratitude, Your Highness," Dimitri said. "But I don't want the money."

Marie smiled tightly, her eyes narrowing in suspicion. She still did not trust this young man. "What do you want, then?"

"Unfortunately," Dimitri mumbled, "nothing you can give."

"Young man! Where did you get that music box?"

Dimitri didn't answer.

"You were the boy, weren't you?" Marie whispered. "The servant boy who got us out? You saved her life, and mine. Then you brought her back to me. And yet you want no reward."

"Not anymore." He bowed, then hurried out the door.

Marie watched him go, a thoughtful look on her face.

At the bottom of the stairs, Dimitri nearly ran into Anastasia.

"Did you collect your reward?" she asked coldly.

"My business is complete," he answered simply.

"Young man," a servant barked. "You will bow and address the Princess as 'Your Highness.'"

Anastasia blushed. "No, that's not necessary—"

"Please, Your Highness," Dimitri said, and bowed. "I'm glad you found what you were looking for."

"Yes, I'm glad you did, too," Anastasia replied.

"Well, then . . . good-bye. Your Highness."

"Good-bye," she whispered softly.

❁

"You're making a terrible mistake!" Vladimir exclaimed.

Dimitri had come to tell his best friend good-bye.

75

"Trust me. This is the one thing I'm doing right." He shook Vladimir's hand. "If you're ever in St. Petersburg again, look me up."

Pooka whimpered at his feet.

Dimitri scratched the puppy's nose. "So long, mutt."

❖

Anastasia peeked through a set of velvet curtains that night. A sea of dazzling couples waltzed across the ballroom.

No one had ever thrown a party for her before. Not even for her birthday. At least not that she could remember.

She could hardly believe all these important people had come to see her! Her eyes scanned the crowd. She wondered if maybe, just maybe . . .

"He's not there," Marie said over her shoulder.

"Oh, I know he's not," Anastasia said quickly. "He—" Embarrassed, she tried to ignore the hot blush stinging her cheeks. "Who's not there, Grandmama?"

But Marie knew better. "The young man who found a music box," she replied.

"He's too busy spending his reward money as fast as he can," Anastasia said scornfully.

Marie looked at her beloved granddaughter, then

gestured to the crowd. "Look at them dance!" she said. "Like me, they're so thrilled to welcome you, and honor you, and cherish you."

"I know," Anastasia said sadly. "It makes me . . . so happy."

She turned to her grandmother, who did not look at all convinced. "No—it was finding you again, finding what I could not even remember I had lost, that has made me happy," Anastasia explained.

She threw her arms around Marie, and the two embraced each other tightly.

Tears filled Marie's eyes. As painful as it was, she knew she had to tell Anastasia the truth about Dimitri. She stepped back, looked at her beautiful grand-daughter, and sighed.

"He didn't take the money," Marie said.

Anastasia gasped. "He . . . didn't . . ."

"He didn't take it," Marie said again. "And now you will have to decide what to do, my darling. There is no place for him out there in that glittering crowd. No place for him beside the Grand Duchess Ana-stasia."

Anastasia's mind was a whirl of confused feelings.

She'd found what she'd been searching for. A home. Family. Love. But so much more.

Tonight she wore a beautiful gown, a crown on

her head. People called her "Your Highness" and served her from silver platters. It was enough to make any girl feel like a princess.

Yet *inside* she felt like the same girl she'd always been.

Now she knew her real name. She could recite her whole family tree.

But who am I? she wondered. She still had so many unanswered questions.

Marie broke into her thoughts. "Whatever you choose, I will hold you in my heart always," she said gently.

"Grandmama, can't you tell me—"

But Marie was gone. Anastasia pushed back the curtain to look at the crowd once again.

Just then Pooka started barking. Loudly. Very loudly. Something was wrong.

She peered out into the darkness. "Pooka?" she called. Anastasia turned and saw him dart through the terrace doors.

When the puppy didn't answer, Anastasia gathered the skirts of her gown and hurried onto the terrace.

"Dimitri, is that you?" she asked hopefully, stepping into the garden.

❀

Dimitri stood in line at the train station, staring at the ground. Anya . . . Anastasia . . . was he right to leave? To let her think he didn't care? He wanted her to regain the crown that was rightfully hers—didn't he?

"Next," the ticket agent said.

Dimitri stepped up to the counter. He opened his mouth to speak, but no sound came out. What should he do? He took a deep breath . . .

"One ticket to St. Petersburg," he said finally.

❁

Anastasia hurried through the dark garden. It wasn't like Pooka to hide from her. Where could he be? She followed the sound of his barking.

The garden grew darker and darker as she moved farther away from the lights and music of the party and deeper into the topiary garden. Shadows slithered threateningly behind her.

Pooka suddenly stopped barking. The silence was overwhelming. Anastasia felt a chill run down her spine. She could feel it—something was not right in the garden.

Pooka appeared and started barking at the bushes. Anastasia whirled around. *That bush wasn't there before*, she thought. It was almost as if the bushes were moving—following her. Frantic, she spun around. They were moving closer!

"An-a-sta-sia," a strange voice called.

What was that? Anastasia grabbed her skirts and ducked through a small opening in the bushes, with Pooka right on her heels. She pushed through the greenery to find herself by the river.

A twisted figure stood on a bridge, clutching a glowing object.

He faced Anastasia and gave a sweeping bow.

"Your Imperial Highness," he said in a mocking tone. "Look what ten years has done to us: You a beautiful young flower. And me a rotting corpse."

Anastasia stared at the man. "That face!" she whispered. Why was it so familiar?

"Last seen at a party like this one," Rasputin replied.

"A curse . . ." Anastasia said, remembering.

Rasputin raised the glowing vial. "Followed by a tragic night on the ice, remember?" he bellowed, firing a stream of crackling smoke from the reliquary. The bridge was instantly covered in a sheet of glittering ice. The smiling stone cherubs that decorated the bridge were turned into hideous demons with long teeth and grotesque grins.

Anastasia was thrown to the ground by the blast. But despite her shock and pain, the memories came flooding back as she struggled to her feet.

An elegant party. A young girl with long red

curls dancing with her handsome father. An evil holy man, shouting a curse to destroy the entire Romanov family!

"Rasputin!" she cried.

"Rasputin!" he replied. "Destroyed by your despicable family! But what goes around comes around!"

He let out a sinister laugh as he raised the reliquary above his head. He stepped toward her, and the smell of his rotting flesh stung her nostrils. Anastasia stood, frozen with fear.

Smoke billowed out of the reliquary. Suddenly, the minions materialized. Swarming toward Anastasia, they knocked her off balance and began spinning her around in circles. They tore at her lovely gown and swatted the crown off her head. They began inching the dizzy girl toward the edge of the bridge. Anastasia would surely fall to her death in the waters below!

Images of Anastasia's family filled her mind. The family she should have grown up with. The family she'd never see again. Anger filled her heart. And anger gave her courage. She fought back, and struck out at the minions, which squealed and disappeared into puffs of black smoke.

Bartok the bat had seen enough. Turning to Rasputin he said, "You're on your own, sir. This can only end in tears." He flew off, landing on a nearby statue of Pegasus, the winged horse, perched high atop a column.

Anastasia stepped forward. "I'm not afraid of you!" she shouted at the surprised Rasputin.

"I can fix that!" he snarled. "Care for a little swim under the ice?"

He raised the reliquary again. Smoke shot out and the once sturdy bridge began to crack into pieces. A blast of ice and snow knocked Anastasia off her feet. She struggled, but began to slide off the bridge.

"Say your prayers, Anastasia!" Rasputin cackled with glee. "No one can save you now!"

"Wanna bet?" a voice cried out.

It was Dimitri!

Rasputin spun around. Dimitri charged at him, punching him in the face. Rasputin turned and raised the reliquary once more. It blasted the bridge again, and Anastasia slipped even further.

"Anya!" shouted Dimitri. He reached out to save her.

Anastasia struggled to grab his outstretched hand. "Dimitri!" she cried.

Rasputin stared down at them. "How enchanting!" he cackled. "Together again—for the *last* time."

He fired again, this time right at Dimitri. A swarm of minions attacked him and lifted him into the air— right onto the statue of Pegasus.

Suddenly the statue sprang to life. It leaped off the column with Dimitri on its back. The Pegasus was alive—and very, very angry.

The horse bucked Dimitri off its back. Dimitri flew through the air, landing hard upon the bridge. Neighing and rearing wildly, the Pegasus began attacking him. Dimitri struggled to roll away from the pounding hooves.

Meanwhile, Anastasia climbed back up the bridge. Rasputin looked down upon her and smiled a hideous smile. "Finally, the last Romanov death!" he shouted with evil glee. He grabbed the Princess with both hands. "*Dasvidanya,* Your Highness," he sneered, using the Russian word for "good-bye." He shoved her back over the side of the bridge.

Anastasia grabbed the bridge desperately with both hands. If only Rasputin could be distracted for an instant!

As if reading his mistress's mind, Pooka darted forward and sank his teeth into Rasputin's ankle. Rasputin screamed in rage, then turned back to look at Anastasia.

Rasputin saw nothing but a cloud of smoke and ice.

Anastasia was gone.

Chapter Eleven

Despite his fall, Dimitri struggled to his feet. "Anya!" he cried. Without thinking of his own safety, he leaped off the bridge in search of her.

"Stop him!" Rasputin thundered. The Pegasus charged after Dimitri, who grabbed the horse's reins. They flew in the air for a moment, then Dimitri fell, disappearing into the smoke.

Rasputin scanned the scene on the bridge with a satisfied expression. He raised his fist into the air. "Long live the Romanovs!" he sneered.

"I couldn't have said it better myself," Anastasia said, as she stepped out of the smoke and shadows.

Rasputin's mouth fell open. She lunged at him, knocking him down. The reliquary fell from his hand and rolled across the bridge.

Rasputin lurched forward and grabbed on to the glowing vial. He shot a powerful surge of minions at Anastasia, and she tumbled backward.

Rasputin raised the reliquary again to finish Anastasia off for good . . .

. . . and Pooka grabbed it in his mouth! But then he dropped it, and the vial landed right by Anastasia's foot.

Rasputin cowered in fear. Anastasia stared deep into his eyes. Then she heard a whinny, and turned. Dimitri lay motionless beneath the huge Pegasus on the broken bridge.

"This is for my family!" she shouted in fury, and stomped the reliquary.

Then her thoughts turned to everything else this evil man had taken from her.

"This is for stealing my childhood!" She brought her foot down on it again, hard. The Pegasus crumbled to pieces.

"Give it back!" Rasputin screamed in fury.

"And this is for Dimitri!" she bellowed, bringing her foot down yet again. *"Dasvidanya!"*

KABOOM! The reliquary exploded, splashing

Rasputin with an eerie green light. Rasputin screamed. Anastasia watched in shock and horror as the light coursed through his body like an electric current. The minions, attracted to Rasputin like moths to a flame, began circling around him faster and faster.

Rasputin's skin glowed with a fiery light. Then it began to shimmer. If it weren't so hideous, it might have been beautiful. Anastasia watched, awestruck, as his skin began to bubble, ooze, and finally melt off his body, leaving nothing but a shrieking, rattling skeleton.

The skeleton fell to pieces and crumbled to dust as the minions flew away.

Moments later, a soft evening breeze swept away the last wisps of smoke. The Eiffel Tower came into view, pointing toward the stars.

Anastasia hurried over to the still body of Dimitri. With a heavy heart, she gently stroked his hair.

Suddenly, he groaned!

"Dimitri!" Anastasia gasped.

"Ouch!" said Dimitri. Then he slowly rose to his feet and smiled. "I know, I know. All men are babies."

They moved closer together.

Anastasia spoke first. "I thought you were going to St. Peters—"

"I was . . . " Dimitri replied.

"You didn't take the money," Anastasia said.

"I couldn't," Dimitri admitted. "Because . . . I . . . I . . ." he stuttered.

But Anastasia knew what he was trying to say.

"Me too," she said with a gentle smile.

They leaned forward, closed their eyes . . .

. . . and Pooka started barking.

The two parted to find the playful puppy wagging his tail, with Anastasia's crown in his mouth.

Dimitri sighed in resignation. "They're waiting for you," he said and sadly handed his princess her crown.

❁

In the palace, Marie and Sophie sat in a small room. On the table sat a hat box, Anastasia's crown, and a note. Sophie stared at the note as the tears streamed down her plump face. But they were tears of joy. "It seems like only yesterday she came here," she said.

"At least we had that yesterday," Marie replied. "Now *she* has her tomorrow." She stared out the window, and dashed a single tear from her cheek before Sophie could see. She turned to her cousin. "Dry your eyes now. We have guests."

Anastasia had returned her crown.

It appeared that Dimitri had found his reward after all.

And Anastasia had found a home.

The old woman smiled a bittersweet smile as she gazed out the window.

She knew that Anastasia and Dimitri were out there, somewhere, beneath the starry night sky.

Anastasia has chosen wisely, Marie thought. *And so has her young man.*

They knew that the greatest treasure—the one more precious than rubles or golden crowns—was love.